TO THOSE WHO READ THIS TALE, NOTICE IS HEREBY GIVEN:

Under full penalty of law, exaggeration is forbidden in the state of Texas. No Texan may decorate a plain fact — except if that person is an elected official, or anyone who has ever ridden a horse. In such cases, all exaggeration must be restricted to the first twenty-four hours past sunrise.

For my husband, Rick—my own Charlie Doughpuncher—with all my love —A.I.

To Jessie and her Doughpuncher! —K.H.

Text copyright © 2014 by The Anne Isaacs 2004 Trust
Jacket art and interior illustrations
copyright © 2014 by Kevin Hawkes
All rights reserved.
Published in the United States by
Schwartz & Wade Books,
an imprint of Random House Children's Books,
a division of Random House, Inc., New York.
Schwartz & Wade Books and the colophon
are trademarks of Random House, Inc.
Educators and librarians, for a variety of teaching tools,
visit us at RHTeachersLibrarians.com
Library of Congress Cataloging-in-Publication Data
Isaacs, Anne. [Back at the ranch]
Meanwhile, back at the ranch / Anne Isaacs ; Kevin Hawkes.—
1st ed. p. cm.

Summary: In 1870, Tulip Jones, a wealthy, self-reliant widow from
England, acquires the By-Golly Gully Ranch in Texas and soon finds
herself saddled with 1000 suitors. ISBN 978-0-375-86745-3 (hc)
ISBN 978-0-375-96745-0 (lib. bdg.) — ISBN 978-0-375-98788-5
(ebook) [1. Ranch life—Texas—Fiction. 2. Courtship—Fiction.
3. Texas—History—1865–1950—Fiction. 4. Humorous stories.
5. Tall tales.] I. Hawkes, Kevin, ill. II. Title.
PZ7.1762 Bac 2013 [E]—dc23 2011046490
The text of this book is set in Celestia Antiqua.
The illustrations were rendered in Open acrylics and
Prismacolor pencil on Bristol board.
MANUFACTURED IN CHINA
10 9 8 7 6 5 4 3 2 1
First Edition
Random House Children's Books supports the
First Amendment and celebrates the right to read.

Meanwhile, Back at The Ranch

by **Anne Isaacs**

illustrated by **Kevin Hawkes**

schwartz & wade books · new york

On the Fourth of July 1870, the widow Tulip Jones of Greater Bore, England, inherited thirty-five million dollars and a ranch at By-Golly Gully, Texas. She moved there at once. She brought two trunks of tea and her twelve pet tortoises: January, February, March—and so on, in order of age, down to little December, who was not much bigger than the period at the end of this sentence. Three servants came along as ranch hands—Linsey, Woolsey, and Calico.

They arrived in the middle of the hottest summer Texas had ever known. By-Golly Gully was so hot that chickens laid hard-boiled eggs, and lizards hobbled around on tiny stilts to avoid burning their feet on the ground.

"Grab your hoes, girls!" said Tulip Jones. "We're going to plant a garden."

She soon found that everything raised on Texas soil grows faster, bigger, and better than anywhere else. Linsey, Woolsey, and Calico had to climb a ladder to pick tomatoes. Potatoes got so big that it took only seven of them to make a dozen. A single watermelon fed everyone on the ranch for a month; afterward, they used the hollow rind as a hay shed.

Not surprisingly, Widow Jones's tortoises also grew to amazing proportions. Within a month, even little December measured six feet from his tail to his nose. Now, you might think their size would slow them down, but facts are otherwise. The bigger those tortoises grew, the faster they ran—until eventually, they could outgallop any racehorse.

"A tortoise can do whatever a horse can, only better!" declared Tulip Jones proudly. She ordered saddles and reins and rode her pets all over the prairie.

"This peaceful life suits me just fine," Widow Jones would say, while she and her ranch hands drank tea and gazed at the summer sky. But it didn't stay peaceful very long.

For word spread as fast as prairie wind that a widow with thirty-five million dollars had settled on By-Golly Ranch. Soon every unmarried man in Texas hoped to marry Tulip Jones—and in 1870, every man in Texas *was* unmarried.

Before long, a line of suitors stretched from By-Golly Ranch to the town of Toad Crossing, a mile down the road.

With one thousand men dropping by for tea every day, Widow Jones had to hire Charlie Doughpuncher, a baker from Abilene, to bake tea cakes, biscuits, cookies, and pies.

Each night, after all the suitors had left, Tulip Jones would sit in the kitchen and complain to Charlie, while he mixed the next day's bread and muffins.

"That Tumbleweed Thompson is so clumsy he couldn't hit the ground with his lasso," she told Charlie one night. "And Big Toe Anderson has nothing on his mind but his hat!"

"Try this," Charlie said comfortingly, and he offered her a blueberry scone fresh out of the oven.

"I'm not looking for a husband," Widow Jones explained to one suitor after another. "I like it fine on my own." Still, the men kept coming. And coming.

But when Sheriff Arroyo and his brother Spit showed up, all the other suitors stepped back to let them pass. The Arroyo brothers were the leaders of the infamous Hole in the Pants Gang, who had been terrorizing ranchers and stealing cattle for years. Because the sheriff ran the gang, it didn't seem likely they would ever be brought to justice.

Sheriff and Spit Arroyo marched up to
Widow Jones with grins as wide as their
hats, determined to make her marry one
of them. They didn't care which one, for
they planned to grab her money and run
off to Mexico—without her—the minute
the wedding was over.

"You'd be the safest lady in Texas if you
married me," Sheriff Arroyo lied.

"Riprocious!" said Spit.

Tulip Jones recoiled in horror.

"Those Arroyos are so mean, dynamite would hide from them," she told Charlie Doughpuncher that night, while he frosted gingersnaps.

Charlie set a pile of cookies before the widow. "Try this," he said, his kind face wrinkling with concern.

"I don't think I can stand another day of these suitors, Charlie," said Tulip Jones. "I've got to find a way to get rid of them!"

All that night, she paced across the porch, munching on Charlie's cookies and thinking. By the time the sun rose, she had a plan.

"Girls, this is the last day you'll have to wash dishes for a thousand men," she told her ranch hands at breakfast. "I'm going to get rid of the suitors, for good!"

"Hooray!" shouted Linsey, Woolsey, and Calico.

"I'll give the suitors a task and promise to marry the man who succeeds," Widow Jones explained. "But it will be an *impossible* task," she added gleefully, "so everyone will fail!"

"But what if someone should succeed?" asked Calico.

"Succeed?" Tulip Jones snorted in disgust. "Those men are so weak they couldn't lift their own shadows."

Still, the ranch hands weren't convinced.

"We won't have any peace at this ranch until Widow Jones gets married," Linsey said as she washed teacups.

"Or until all one thousand cowboys get married," added Woolsey as she dried the cups. "If only we could find a thousand brides for them—fast!"

"Maybe we can," said Calico with a sly grin as she set clean cups on a shelf. "I've got an idea!"

Later that day, the Pony Express carried a notice from By-Golly Ranch, to be printed in every newspaper in America:

Brides wanted! 1,000 cowboys available! Free to good homes! Lariat and hat included! All guaranteed, purebred Texans! Limited offer; act fast! Reply to By-Golly Ranch, Texas.

back at By-Golly Ranch, Widow Jones announced her challenge: "I'll marry the man who can make the Rio Grande River flow backwards!"

Nine hundred and fifty men gave up on the spot and left the ranch. But the rest were undaunted. Within an hour, fifty suitors set out for the Rio Grande River.

"This ranch will be a heap quieter from now on,"
Tulip Jones told Charlie Doughpuncher cheerfully.
"Try this," Charlie replied with a smile, as he pulled
a blueberry tart from the oven.

But before the day was out—to the astonishment of Widow Jones—
four men succeeded in making the Rio Grande flow backwards.

Big Toe Anderson piled sand in the shallowest tributary to make
a dam. The water rose and rose on the upriver side until it started to
push itself backwards.

Tumbleweed Thompson bought every loaf of bread in Texas and lured ten million ducks downstream with bread crumbs. As twenty million webbed feet paddled hard against the current, they slowed the mighty river, stopped it—and finally pushed it backwards.

Spit and Sheriff Arroyo found an easier solution: they dug a small ditch next to the river and diverted a trickle of water into it, flowing in the opposite direction. "You didn't say how *much* had to flow backwards," the sheriff reminded Widow Jones, and she had to admit that this was true.

"Guess I need another task," the widow said, fighting discouragement. She thought quickly and handed each man a pail, saying, "I'll marry the man who can fill this with stars!"
Night was falling as the four suitors rode off.

Meanwhile,

in cities and towns all over America, one thousand hopeful brides-to-be sewed wedding gowns and veils and boarded trains bound for Texas.

Next morning, the Arroyo brothers
returned to By-Golly Ranch alone. Each
held a pail filled with small rocks.
"Caught ourselves some shootin' stars,
Widder!" called Sheriff Arroyo.

"You can't prove those rocks fell from the sky," protested Widow Jones.

"You can't prove they didn't," replied the sheriff.

"Riprocious!" shouted Spit.

Once again, Widow Jones had to give in.

"Help me, Charlie!" she cried, racing into the kitchen. "I need another task, fast! And this time, it has to be truly impossible."

"Try this," said Charlie, showing her the front page of that morning's *Abilene Gazette*.

HOLE IN THE PANTS GANG STILL AT LARGE
President Grant Says Catching Gang Is
"Challenge of the Century"

"Why, Charlie, what a wonderful idea!" said Tulip Jones. She ran back outside and announced: "I'll marry the man who puts every one of the Hole in the Pants Gang in jail!"

Sheriff's and Spit Arroyo's jaws dropped so wide that several young bats mistook their mouths for caves, and flew in to hang upside down on their teeth.

"Every—last—one—?" spluttered Sheriff Arroyo, choking on bats.

"Riprocious!" shouted Spit. He howled with laughter; and the sound was so bone-chilling that coyotes all over Texas covered their ears.

At that, the Arroyo brothers rode off; and for the rest of the night, Tulip Jones paced across her porch, sharing her worries with Charlie.

"Those sneaky Arroyo brothers are bound to come up with some kind of trick," she said. "Oh, what can I do?"

Charlie offered plenty of strawberry shortcake and sympathy, but neither he nor Tulip Jones got a wink of sleep that night.

at the Abilene station, one thousand brides got off the train and marched to By-Golly Ranch. Their white gowns and long white veils blew out behind them.

"Is it snowing—or am I seeing ghosts?" Widow Jones asked her ranch hands the next morning as the brides appeared on the horizon.

"Ma'am, I can explain," said Linsey, and told her about the newspaper notice.

"Thank you, girls! You've given me a splendid idea," said Tulip Jones. "Saddle up the tortoises!" she added as she ran to welcome the brides. "We're all going for a ride."

Minutes later, the tortoises galloped out of By-Golly Ranch with a thousand brides on their backs while Widow Jones shouted instructions: "Take out your needles and thread, ladies. . . ."

In Dungaree Canyon, the Hole in the Pants Gang were fast
asleep when Widow Jones and the thousand brides showed up.
On the way there, the women had stitched together their wedding
veils to make a five-mile-long net.

The moment they arrived, they raced along the cliff edge, dragging the huge net over Dungaree Canyon and sealing off every possible path of escape.

When Sheriff Arroyo, Spit, and the gang woke up, they found themselves surrounded.

"Don't make us get married!" the gang begged, trembling in terror. They burst into tears. "Throw us in a swamp with alligators—make us eat lizard guts—we'll even take a bath! Only don't make us get married!"

"Riprocious!" sobbed Spit Arroyo.

"We'll do anything you ask!" pleaded the sheriff, more desperate than a coyote that's just swallowed a cactus. "Anything!"

"Anything?" said Widow Jones with a grin.

Later that day, at the Toad Crossing Jail, Sheriff Arroyo, Spit, and every member of the gang raced into jail cells. Widow Jones cheerfully locked them in and telegraphed the governor to send a new sheriff to Toad Crossing and a justice of the peace to By-Golly Ranch.

"Wedding at By-Golly Ranch tonight," she telegraphed. "Everyone in Texas invited!"

meanwhile,

Linsey, Woolsey, and Calico raced from
ranch to ranch, all across Texas, telling
cowboys that a thousand brides were waiting
for them at By-Golly Ranch.

Meanwhile, back at By-Golly Ranch, Charlie Doughpuncher poured seven thousand eggs, ten thousand gallons of milk, two hundred lemons, one ton of butter, two tons of sugar, forty pails of baking powder, and four thousand pounds of flour into a mile-wide meteor crater, and mixed the batter by paddling around in a canoe. Then he left the cake to bake in the Texas sun. It rose and rose, until the top climbed out of sight above the clouds.

It was impossible to move the cake, so as soon as the justice of the peace had married them, all two thousand newlyweds grabbed forks and gobbled the cake from bottom to top, until every last crumb was gone.

   While evening settled on the land like a purple wedding veil,
the newlyweds thanked Widow Jones one by one and rode off
from By-Golly Ranch. Linsey, Woolsey, and Calico left, too; for
the three ranch hands had caught "marrying fever" and found
husbands of their own.

It was midnight when the last couple left and Tulip Jones went into the kitchen for her nightly talk with Charlie Doughpuncher.

But Charlie wasn't there.

Tulip Jones ran all over the ranch, searching, but he wasn't anywhere. "I should have thought of this," the widow told herself sadly. "With the suitors gone, he must have figured I'd have no more need of him." In the hall, the grandfather clock ticked. Far off, a coyote pack howled out its song, and the melody went riding up and down the hills. "But I do need him!" Tulip Jones declared. Tears came to her eyes.

Suddenly she heard a wagon and saw a lantern swinging from the top rail.

"Charlie!" she cried, lighting up like a firefly as she ran out to meet him. "I'm so glad to see you!"

"Try this," Charlie said. He smiled as he handed her a small box.

Inside was a wedding ring.

And back at the ranch, they lived happily ever after.

The
End